MORE TALES OF
faraway folk

MORE TALES OF

faraway folk

CHOSEN AND RETOLD BY

BABETTE DEUTSCH AND
AVRAHM YARMOLINSKY

PICTURES BY JANINA DOMANSKA

HARPER & ROW, PUBLISHERS
NEW YORK, EVANSTON, AND LONDON

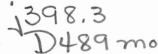

MORE TALES OF FARAWAY FOLK

Library of Congress catalog card number: 63–15321

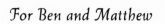

For Ben and Matthew

Contents

Foreword

If you know the first book of tales of faraway folk, this Foreword has nothing new to tell you. But if you are starting in with MORE TALES, then you should hear what it says.

On the shores of icy seas, at the edge of forests where wild creatures lurk, in the shadow of savage crags, and on broad plains where as far as the eye can see the only billows are those of the wheat in the wind live people with few books or none. They work hard, hunting, trapping, and fishing, or caring for crops, or minding their herds on the hills. But when night comes, they gather round the fire, in their huts or tents, or perhaps out under the stars, and tell stories. One northern tribe has a saying that in ancient times, to keep men from being weary-hearted, a kind god created the storyteller. He is an important figure, but most of the older people can relate the tales, and the younger ones soon learn them. In these pages you will find set down a few that they especially like to tell and to hear.

MORE TALES OF
faraway folk

Why the Fish Do Not Speak

The Finns call their marshy northern country Suomi, but we call it Finland. That sounds like a good name for a land of lakes full of finny folk. No wonder the fish swim into their stories.

This story is told about the time when no one and nothing knew how to speak. The birds had no songs. The animals had no cries. The waters flowed and the winds blew, but they made no noise. Even man did not have any language at all.

Luckily there was someone who could mend matters.

1

That someone was the Master of Song himself, the powerful Vainamoinen.

He sat down on the only place big enough to hold him: a mountain that was not too high and not too low. Naturally he had his harp with him. He held the harp in one hand, and with the other he lightly struck the strings. At the sound man pricked up his ears. And so did every other creature on earth or in the sky. And so did the winds and the waters and the trees.

"Come!" shouted Vainamoinen. "Come, each and all, and choose the language that suits you best."

The wind wanted to choose the loud roar and rattle and rumble of Vainamoinen's big boots as he hoisted himself a little farther up in his mountain seat. But the thunder got first choice. So the language of the thunder is much noisier than the wind's, but it never talks for as long a time as the wind does. The river that wound about the foot of the mountain at once decided that the rushing swish of Vainamoinen's cloak as he bent over his harp made a delicious sound. So rivers have been using that language ever since. The trees thought that the rustle of Vainamoinen's sleeves was the simplest speech for those whose lips were leaves. That is why trees always rustle when they talk. The

birds, of course, found no speech pleasing until Vainamoinen played a little melody on his harp. Then the
lark and the nightingale and the rest of the singing
birds found their proper languages. All the creatures
of the field and the wood, the desert and the jungle
gathered about the Master of Song. As they listened
to him each discovered a way of whistling or whis-
pering, of humming or drumming, of barking or
squawking, of yelling or bellowing that seemed a
proper language.

As for man, he learned all the different sounds that
Vainamoinen's garments made as he moved this way
or that. And he learned all the tones of Vainamoinen's
harp strings, whether he was striking them or stilling
them. And so man speaks many, many languages, each
one of them wonderful in a special way. And when he
wants to, man can make even better music than the
birds do, and his music sets the heart dancing almost
as if the Master of Song were there himself.

Vainamoinen was heartily pleased. And so were all
those who now began to talk to one another, each in its
own way.

But while everything on earth and above the earth
had been listening to Vainamoinen and deciding what

language to choose for its own, the fish were quite helpless. There they were, swimming about, and they understood very well that something remarkable was going on. But they had no idea what it could be. The excitement ran so high that at great risk they even stuck their heads out of the water. It was just for a moment, and they didn't dare stick them out far, certainly not far enough so that their ears were able to catch what was going on. But their eyes peered above the water just long enough for them to get a glimpse of the other creatures. There those others were, all of them who had just picked out their very own languages and now were practicing them, chattering and jabbering away as fast as ever they could.

The fish could see all the beaks and all the mouths opening and shutting, opening and shutting, opening and shutting. But of course the fish, with their ears under water, couldn't hear a sound. Nevertheless, when they saw all those mouths opening and shutting, opening and shutting, opening and shutting, they made up their minds that they must join in and behave just as the other creatures did. So, not knowing any better, the fish began to open and shut their mouths. Not a sound came out of them.

4

WHY THE FISH DO NOT SPEAK

If you watch the fish you will see that they keep on opening and shutting, opening and shutting, their mouths to this day. And to this very day they do not make a sound!

The Bat

The people of that part of central Asia called the Altai live among high mountains, rushing rivers, and steep ravines. Some of their stories are about how this gigantic landscape was formed. They like to hear about the birds and the beasts, too, especially if the creature is as sly as the one in this tale.

As everybody knows, the bat sleeps all day and flies only at night. But it was not always so. Time was when the bat flew in the daylight as well.

Now it happened once long and long ago that the bat was flying about in the sunshine and he met a hawk.

7

"Worthy Bat," said the hawk, "I have been looking for you for three years."

"Well, well," said the bat. "And what do you want of me?"

"All the birds paid their taxes long ago," answered the hawk. "Only you have not paid yours."

"I?" cried the bat with a squeak of astonishment. "But why under the sun should I? Am I a bird?"

With these words he dropped to the ground and ran quickly across the grass on his four feet. He was soon out of sight.

"Indeed," the hawk said to himself, "the bat is no bird: he is a beast!"

The bat ran on till he reached the woods. In a grove of pine trees he stopped to rest. It was high noon, the sun was hot, and the shade of the pine trees was cool and pleasant.

While the bat rested there, he heard a rustling in the underbrush. A silver fox came trotting toward him.

"Good day to you, Worthy Bat," said the fox. "I am heartily glad to see you. I have been looking for you these seven years."

"Well, well, think of that!" said the bat. "What do you want of me?"

"All the beasts have paid their taxes," answered the fox. "Only you have failed to pay yours."

"I!" cried the bat with a squeak of astonishment. "But why under the sun should I? Am I a beast?"

With these words the bat unfolded his wings and soared away high over the tops of the pine trees.

"Indeed!" the fox said to himself. "The bat is no beast: he is a bird."

After that the bat never ran anymore, lest he should run into the fox. His legs withered up with fear. And he did not fly by daylight anymore, lest he meet the hawk on the paths of the sky. But from that day to this he hangs upside down by his tiny claws all day, and he uses his wings only in the dark when the hawk is asleep.

Why the Bear's Tail Is Short

*If you know the stories of Hans Christian Andersen, you have heard
something about the Lapps, who live in the far north of Europe. There
are not many of them. They hunt and herd the reindeer, whose flesh is
their meat and whose pelts provide them with warm clothing, socks, and
shoes. Huddled around the fire they try to while away the long, cold
nights by telling tales. One of them is the tale of the bear who lumbers
through the thick forests of Lapland.*

This happened on a very cold day. It was so cold that
no creature dared stir out of its hole but the fox.
The fox was hungry, and so, in spite of the weather,
she went trotting down the road, looking for something

to eat. But there was nothing to be found. Not a bird was flying in the icy wind. Not a mouse was creeping across the snow-covered earth.

Suddenly the fox noticed that a string of sledges, driven by a Lapp, was coming along the road. And on the last of the sledges was a fine load of fish.

At once the fox lay down on the road and stretched out her legs as though she were frozen stiff. When the Lapp drove up, he saw the fox lying there.

"Aha!" he said to himself. "This is a find, indeed! I will take that fox home to my wife, and she will make a coat for our little son out of the foxskin and trim his cap with her bushy tail."

The Lapp halted his reindeer, got down, placed the fox on the sledge behind him, and drove merrily on.

In a little while the fox dropped off the sledge. The Lapp got down, picked her up, and placed her on the second sledge. This went on, with the fox dropping off and the Lapp placing her on the next sledge, until finally the fox found herself on the last sledge of all, which was loaded with fish.

Very quietly and very steadily the fox began to gnaw at the rope that fastened the sledge to the one ahead. At last she gnawed the rope through: the sledge loaded with fish stood still in its tracks, while the rest of the sledges went merrily on. The Lapp did not notice his loss, and the fox settled down for a feast.

When she had eaten her fill, she took a fine fat fish in her mouth so that she would have something for her supper, and trotted off into the forest.

She had not gone far when she met the bear.

"Ah, Mistress Fox," said the bear, "wherever did you get that fine fat fish?"

"I caught it," said the fox.

"And how did you catch it?" asked the bear.

"Oh, it was simple," answered the fox. "I went to the river and stuck in my tail. The fish swam up and caught hold of it, and so I drew my supper out of the water."

"Show me how to do it," begged the bear. For though he had not so thick and bushy a hindpiece as the fox, in those days the bear, too, had a long, respectable tail.

"Come along," said the fox with a grin. She loved a joke better than anything except a good meal.

The fox led the bear to the river and knocked a small hole in the ice for him. The bear stuck his long, respectable tail into the hole and waited for a fish to bite.

"Good fishing," said the fox, and went about her own affairs.

After a while, however, the fox thought that she

really must see how the bear was getting on, and she returned to the river. There stood the bear, patiently holding his long, respectable tail in the ice hole. But, as you know, it was a very cold day, even for Lapland, and by this time the bear's long, respectable tail was frozen fast in the ice.

"Oh, Master Bear!" cried the fox. "Your tail is frozen!"

The bear roared with dismay and tried to pull his long, respectable tail out of the ice hole. The harder he pulled, the louder he roared, but it did not help. At last he managed to get his tail out. But it was not a long, respectable tail any more. Most of it had stuck fast in the ice, and only a short stub remained to him.

From that day to this the bear has worn his tail short. Besides, he has lost his taste for fish. He prefers to eat honey. After all, you can get plenty of honey without having a long, respectable tail.

How the Bee Got His Bumble

Living in the foothills of the Altai Mountains in southern Siberia are
lumberjacks and breeders of cattle. They take for granted the giants
who are apt to stride through their stories. But they have eyes and ears
for very small creatures, too.

Long and long ago there was a seven-headed giant
whose name was Delbegen. He was always looking for something good to put into his seven mouths
and to fill his huge stomach with.

One day Delbegen put out his great forefinger and
beckoned a little bee.

"I have a task for you," Delbegen said to the bee. "Go and bite every creature on earth and find out which has the sweetest flesh. When you have found out, come back and tell me. I will eat that creature whose flesh is sweetest, and no other."

"Just as you say," answered the bee.

So he flew about the earth biting every kind of creature. First he bit a dog, but its flesh was not sweet. Then he bit a cat, but she was not sweet to taste either. Then he bit a horse, but he did not like the flavor. Then he bit a pig. That was a little better. Then he bit a hare, but that had a strange taste. Then he bit a cow, and liked it. Then he bit a deer, but its flavor was wild. At last the bee bit a man.

"Oh!" sang the bee, "man is sweetest, man is sweetest!"

When the man heard this, he fell on his knees before the bee.

"Kind bee!" he begged, "don't sing that song to the giant Delbegen. If he hears you, he will eat us all up!"

But the bee kept on singing:

"Man is sweetest, man is sweetest!"

Now there was a brave man by the name of Sartak-Pai. When Sartak-Pai heard the song, he seized the bee by its wings and tore out its tongue.

16

"Now go to Delbegen with your song!" said Sartak-Pai.

The bee flew away, over the lakes and over the hills, till he came to the seven-headed giant, Delbegen.

"Well," asked Delbegen, cocking his fourteen ears, "whose flesh is sweetest?"

The bee wanted to sing: "Man is sweetest!" But when he opened his mouth without a tongue, he could not sing. Sadly he closed his mouth again. All he could say was:

"Bzzz—bzzz—bzzz—"

And down to this very day the bumblebee cannot say anything else.

Why the Hare's Lip Is Split

Estonia is a small country that juts out into the Gulf of Finland. There are about seven times as many people in the city of New York as there are in the whole of Estonia. Many of the natives get their living by dairy farming and cattle breeding and catching big and little fish, including anchovies. There must be shepherds among them, too. This story that follows is told in more than one place in more than one way, but this is the way the Estonians tell it.

The hare did not always have a split lip. There was a time when all hares had upper lips that were just like those of anybody else. This is the story of what changed their shape.

19

To begin with, the hares were most unhappy. And with good reason. They were always scared. If he saw the shadow of a hawk passing over a meadow, the hare's heart jumped with fright. He would crouch flat on the ground so the hawk should not see him and snatch him up for dinner. If the hare was making his own supper off a fresh lettuce in the garden, he could not enjoy it. He would be trembling with fear that the farmer might come after him with a stick. If a hare found himself in the woods of a fine morning, he would take no pleasure in loping along there. He would look out of the corner of his eye, terrified that a fox might be hiding in the bushes, waiting to pounce on him. Nor was that all. The hare would be scared by the crunch of the carrot he was nibbling. He would be scared by the twitching shadow of his own long ears. And if he fell asleep, he would get no proper rest because he would be scared by his dreams. All hares were like that. They were afraid of everything and everybody. And nobody was afraid of them. They were most unhappy.

One day they gathered in a meadow with a river just beyond it to talk over their miserable lot. There were hundreds and hundreds of them, big hares and little hares, and all of them shivering and shaking with fear. The more they talked, the more things they found to be scared about. The more scared they were, the more they shook and shivered with fright. At last they decided that they could bear this life no longer. They would all go down to the bottom of the meadow, leap into the big river there, and drown themselves. Yes, that was what they would all do. And they would do it at once, before they had time to think.

Now the hares had been so busy talking about their fearful life and making their sad plan to end it that they had not noticed what was happening just beyond their meeting place. They had no idea that there was a sheep pasture between them and the river. But there was. And while the hares had been talking, a flock of sheep had been herded into the pasture and was quietly grazing. The flock had been herded there by sheep dogs, and shepherds were also on hand to give the dogs their orders.

The hares, who had been confabbing with each other, now turned about, and in terrible haste they began loping down toward the river. There were hundreds and hundreds of hares, leaping and jumping and hopping along together.

One of the sheep, disturbed by the commotion, began to run away without even looking up. In all the world there is no creature so silly as a sheep. When the first sheep started off, all the rest of the flock followed her at a huddling run. At once the dogs began running after the sheep, trying to round them up. And the shepherds, knowing that the stupid sheep might easily trample on each other and get hurt, or wander away and get lost, ran after the dogs, urging them on. It was quite a sight. And a noisy affair too, what with the sheep bleating fearfully as they stumbled along, and the dogs barking as they chased the sheep, afraid that they would get away, and the shepherds shouting at the dogs, afraid that they would not head off the flock soon enough.

The hares did not know what it was all about. But they heard terror in the bleating of the sheep, and fear in the shepherds' voices, and they saw plainly that the sheep were running as fast as they could go, the dogs were running after the sheep, the shepherds were running after the dogs. The hares stopped in their tracks to watch this astonishing sight.

And as they looked, they laughed. They sat back on their haunches and just laughed.

"Those sheep are running away from US!" they cried to one another. "We have scared them! WE've scared the dogs! WE've scared the men!!!"

The hares shivered and shook, not with fear but with laughter. They laughed till the tears ran down their cheeks. They laughed till they couldn't speak. They laughed till their lips split.

Ever since, every hare's lip is split in the same way. Of course they forgot all about the plan of drowning themselves, and they never thought of it again.

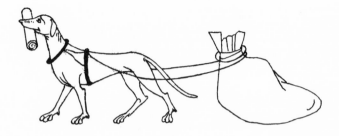

Why the Cat and Dog Cannot Live at Peace

Here is another story that is told in various ways by people living in various countries. And no wonder. The quarrel between cat and dog is an old puzzle. This is the way it is solved by the Ukrainians. Their country lies in the southern part of Russia. It is a region of immense wheatlands, and so it has always been Russia's granary and, indeed, the breadbasket of Europe.

Look at that, now!" a peasant said to the lord of the manor, as a dog chased a cat up a tree and stood below, barking, daring her to come down. "Why is it, master, that cats and dogs are always fighting? Why is it that these two creatures cannot live at peace with one another?"

"Oh, it wasn't always so," replied the lord of the manor, smiling. "I once had a little dog who would not think of fighting with my cat. You should have seen the two of them play together!"

The peasant shook his head.

"Maybe a dog who lives in the manor house sometimes learns how to be polite," he said. "But our dogs are different. And since when haven't cats and dogs been enemies?"

"Since when, indeed?" repeated the lord of the manor, without expecting an answer.

"Listen, and I will tell you," said the peasant.

And this is his story.

Once upon a time there was a terrible famine in the land. Men and animals alike were perishing of hunger. The dog, in despair, pattered off on his four feet to God Himself to beg for bread. God was pleased that the dog had seen fit to come to Him and He gave the creature grain of every sort. Not only that, He gave the dog a piece of writing, beautifully penned by one of His angels, saying: "Whatever your master eats, that he must give you to eat also."

The dog thanked God with many waggings of his tail, harnessed himself to the bag of grain, took the note in his mouth, and returned home. The bag of grain he delivered to his master, who planted it and got a fine crop. The master ate well, and of everything he ate, he gave the dog a fair share. The dog waxed fat and was jolly. And wherever he went, he carried about with him the piece of writing, beautifully penned by one of God's angels.

Now one day the dog was running about the courtyard to see what he could see, when it began to rain. The dog did not mind the wet weather, but he was afraid that the rain might blot the ink on his precious note.

So he ran into the house where the cat was sitting cozily, dreaming of a feast of mice.

"Sister cat," said the dog, "as you see, it is raining. I don't mind the wet weather, but I am afraid it may spoil this precious piece of writing. Please keep it for me. You are one who prefers to stay in the house, where it is cozy and dry. You can keep my note safe."

"Gladly, brother dog," replied the cat, and took the piece of writing. The dog thanked her and ran out again into the yard to see what he could see.

The cat remained in the house, and as it turned

chilly, she crept into the stove, which was still warm, though the fire had gone out.

As the afternoon drew to a close, the mistress of the house bethought her that it was time to prepare dinner. Accordingly, she started to light a fire in the stove. The cat jumped out in a hurry, but she forgot to take the note with her. The piece of writing remained in the stove.

Just then the master of the house came in. He was hungry, and thinking that he would see what there was for dinner, he peeked into the stove. Dinner was not yet in the pot. Indeed, the fire had but just been lit. And there he noticed the dog's precious piece of writing, beautifully penned by one of the angels of God, curling into flame. Before you could say "knife" it was burnt to a crisp.

The master of the house said nothing, but he thought to himself: "Ah, now I need not bother to save some of the best bits for the dog any longer." And he went out to the yard to fetch some more firewood.

In due time dinner was ready, and the master of the house sat down to a hearty meal. He ate well of every dish, but instead of giving the dog his usual share of all the good things, he threw him some bones without any meat on them and some greasy scraps and leftovers that were not at all tasty.

When the dog saw how he was being treated, he went to the cat and said:

"Sister cat, where is the note that I gave you for safe-keeping?"

"Oh," replied the cat, "I was sitting in the stove to warm myself when the mistress came to light the fire. I jumped out of the stove and forgot the note. It must have been burnt."

"Burnt!" howled the dog. "Burnt, do you say!"

And he began barking at the cat in a rage. The cat miaowed, humped her back and spat, and then she ran for her life. And so the pair have been going on ever since.

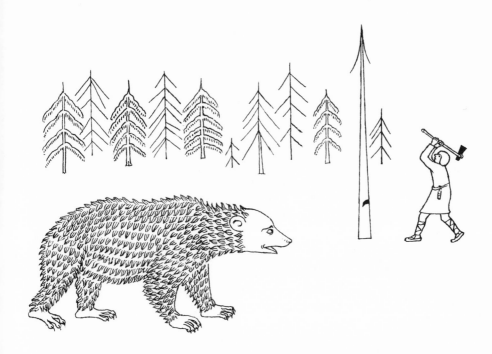

Why the Bear Cannot Play the Kantele

Karelia is a country near Finland, and its people are closely related to the Finns. It is the homeland of the stories that go to make the Kalevala, which means "land of heroes." The stories were recited over and over and handed down from father to son by word of mouth long before they were put in writing. The chief person in the Kalevala is a magician who works wonders by singing to the music of a kind of guitar that is called a kantele. Karelia is a country of many lakes and evergreen forests. Here a woodsman might meet with a bear, as happens in this story.

Once upon a time an old couple lived with their two sons not far from the forest. The elder son was known as Sourpuss Taivo. At heart he was a good

31

fellow, and he was a splendid worker, but he always wore a gloomy look. He never laughed, he never sang. He did his work and he pulled at his pipe. When he went fishing, he was silent. That was all right because he did not scare away the fish. But when he was felling pines in the forest he was silent, too. When he was at home making skis, he was silent. When he was sitting at table with the family, he was silent. That's the sort he was, Sourpuss Taivo.

The younger son was known as Merry Matti. He was a capital fellow. When he was with people, he would joke and laugh. Even when he went fishing, he would sometimes grin to himself. As he worked he sang. He also knew how to play the kantele. This is a musical instrument like a small harp that lies on the knees of the player, who plucks tunes from the metal strings. When Merry Matti began to finger the strings of the kantele and strike up a dance tune, you could not keep quiet: your legs would dance willy-nilly. That's the sort Merry Matti was.

One day Sourpuss Taivo went to the forest to cut wood. When he got there, he left his sledge off to one side, chose a sturdy pine, and began to chop away. The forest was filled with the noise of his axe. There was no other sound, for Sourpuss Taivo was perfectly silent. But the strokes of the axe against the trunk of the pine tree made a tremendous clamor.

Now it happened that a bear had his lair not far from this very pine. The noise awoke the bear.

"Who is making all this racket?" he asked himself grumpily. "A fellow can't sleep!"

He climbed out of his lair and there he saw a man chopping down a tree. The man's cap with its heavy earlaps was pulled down over his forehead. His bushy eyebrows stuck out fiercely. As for the man himself, he was silent. He did not even glance at the bear.

The bear got very angry.

"Why are you making such a noise in my forest?" he demanded. "You woke me up! Deuce take you! Be off with you!"

He made a lunge at Sourpuss Taivo. Such a whack he gave with his great paw that Sourpuss Taivo was almost knocked out. He dropped his axe, rolled over in the snow, and fell onto his sledge.

The sledge gave a sudden lurch and the horse started off. Away he dashed over the snowdrifts, through the trees and across the clearing, and finally brought Sourpuss out of the forest. That's just how it was.

33

At last Sourpuss Taivo reached home. He had no firewood. He had no axe. His jacket was ripped, and he himself was more dead than alive with fright.

What was to be done? Firewood was needed for the stove.

So Merry Matti set off for the forest. He took his kantele, climbed onto the sledge, and drove away. As he drove, he strummed at the kantele and sang a jolly song.

When he got to the forest he saw a pine tree with a deep notch in it and an axe lying nearby on the snow.

"So it's here that Taivo was working," he said.

He left the sledge off to one side and lifted the axe to strike at the trunk. But then he changed his mind.

"Let me play my kantele a bit first," he said. "Then the work will go better." That's the sort he was, Merry Matti.

He sat down on a stump and started to play. The forest was filled with the sound of his kantele. The bear had gone back to his cave to sleep. Now he woke up again.

"Who is making this noise that tickles my ears?" he asked himself.

He lumbered out of his lair and there he saw a man

playing a kantele. The man's cap was perched on the back of his head. His eyebrows were curved above his sparkling eyes. And he was singing.

Willy-nilly, the bear's legs began to dance. The bear capered about in time to the music. He kept on dancing as long as Merry Matti kept on playing.

When Merry Matti stopped, the bear caught his breath.

"Hey, you, man," he said. "Teach me how to play like that. How my cubs would dance!"

"So you want to play the kantele?" said Merry Matti. "That's easy."

He handed the kantele to the bear. But the bear's paws were so thick and clumsy that when he struck the strings only a thick and clumsy sound came from them.

"I'm sorry," said Merry Matti. "That won't do. I must mend your paws. I must make them thinner."

He led the bear to a sturdy pine, split the tree, and set a wedge in the split.

"Now, Master Bear," said Merry Matti, "put your paw in the split and keep it there."

The bear stuck his paw in the split, and Merry Matti hit the wedge. It flew out and the bear's paw stuck fast in the split. The bear roared with pain.

35

"Suffer, suffer," said Merry Matti with a laugh. "Suffer till your paws get thinner. There's no learning without pain."

"I don't want to learn," roared the bear. "I don't want to play the kantele. I want to go home."

"And will you keep on knocking folk about? Will you drive them out of the forest?"

"No, no," roared the bear. "I'll never do it again. Honor bright! Only let me go!"

So Merry Matti drove the wedge into the split again, the bear pulled out his paw, and hobbled back to his lair.

Then Merry Matti went to work and chopped firewood enough and to spare. He loaded the sledge with it, took his kantele, and drove out of the forest, singing as he went. That's the sort he was, Merry Matti.

From that time on, folk went to the forest to chop wood without fear. But the bear never learned to play the kantele.

The Strongest

The mighty Amur River separates the Russian Far East fom China. On both sides of the river dwells a very small tribe of hunters and fishers who call themselves Nanai. They live in crude log cabins and wear clothes made of the pelts of animals and the skins of fish. When they go on a journey or need to carry goods from one place to another, they do not use horses, but harness their dogs to carts or sledges. These animals are sturdy, like their masters.

One winter day some Nanai boys were out sliding on a frozen pond. After a while they got tired of this sport and started to wrestle. A boy named Nameka, a strong fellow, got the best of the biggest boy, whose

39

name was Kurbu. But beating Kurbu was not enough for Nameka. He had to brag about it.

"I'm the strongest!" he shouted. "You must all bow to me."

Just as he said this, Nameka slipped and fell, bashing his nose. It started to bleed.

"You're not the strongest," Kurbu taunted him. "Ice bashed your nose. See, it's bleeding. Bow to Ice."

But Nameka was not so ready to do that.

"Hey, there, Ice!" he called out. "Is there anyone stronger than you?"

"Yes, there is," Ice admitted. "Sun is stronger than me. When it warms up, I just melt. Bow to Sun."

It had been easy enough to question Ice: there it was. But talking to Sun was another matter. The boys tramped for a long time. Finally they came within earshot of Sun.

"Hey, there, Father Sun," Nameka called out. "I got the best of Kurbu. Ice got the best of me, you melt Ice, so you are strongest. We have come to bow to you."

Sun listened. Sun thought. Sun thought again.

"Cloud is stronger than me," Sun told Nameka. "When it comes between me and the earth, my rays can't pierce it, and earth shivers with cold."

At once the boys set off to find Cloud. They climbed and climbed till they neared the top of a high mountain. They were wrapped in a cold, wet fog. They went on climbing. By the time they finally reached Cloud, they were worse than wet: they were crusted with rime.

"Hey, there, Mother Cloud," Nameka called out. "Listen! I am stronger than Kurbu, Ice is stronger than me, Sun is stronger than Ice, you are stronger than all! We've come to bow to you."

Just as Cloud was about to answer him there was a shrill whistling and swirling and Wind shredded Cloud to tatters. Only a moment ago it had been chilly and wet, and you could not see two paces ahead. Suddenly it was warm and bright, Sun began to shine, there was a rainbow, and there before your eyes spread the whole of the Amur River, from its headwaters to its mouth.

"Hey, there, Wind," Nameka called out. "Listen! I thrashed Kurbu, Ice gave me a nosebleed, Sun melted Ice, Cloud blotted out Sun, you shredded Cloud to tatters. So you are stronger than all of us. I must bow to you."

Nameka was about to bow from the waist when Kurbu stepped in front of him and addressed Wind.

"See here, Wind," he cried. "Can you move Mountain from his place?"

Wind did not bother to answer. He started blowing. But no matter how he puffed out his cheeks, Mountain stood as before. Only a few grains of sand flew from his shoulder.

"Well," said Nameka, "you'll have to be at it a long time, Wind, if you're going to move Mountain. It turns out that Mountain is stronger than all."

The boys bowed to Mountain.

As Nameka lifted his head he said, marveling: "Mountain, Mountain, are you really the strongest in the whole world?"

Mountain growled. Mountain thought. Mountain spoke:

"No," he said, honestly. "Tree is stronger than me. It thrusts its roots into my back and makes a crack in me."

Nameka bowed to Tree.

"Hey, there, Tree," he called out. "I thrashed Kurbu, Ice gave me a nosebleed, Sun melted Ice, Cloud blotted out Sun, Wind shredded Cloud to tatters, Mountain stood out against Wind, but you are stronger than Mountain. It's true, then, Tree, you are strongest of all!"

"Yes," Tree rustled proudly. "I am strongest!"

Then Nameka's eyes fell on something that shone at Tree's foot. It was a woodsman's ax.

"You are not!" cried Nameka. And he lifted the woodsman's ax and felled Tree.

Then all of them: Mountain, Wind, Cloud, Sun, Ice, bowed to Nameka. Ever since, Man has been known to be strongest of all.

Master and Man

The steep Caucasus mountains lie between the Black Sea and the Caspian, and south of the range lies Armenia, from which this story comes. There is a legend that it was here that Noah's ark came to rest. Another legend has it that the Garden of Eden was located in the valley of a river which flows along the boundary between Turkey and Armenia. But this story is not about Eden. It is about a world where men labor in the sweat of their faces.

Once upon a time there were two brothers who lived together. They were very poor. The elder brother decided to mend matters.

"I am going to hire myself out as a farm hand," he

said to the younger brother. "You stay here and take care of things at home. When I have earned my wages I will bring them back with me, and we shall live well."

And so it was arranged. The younger brother stayed behind to look after their little house. The elder went off and hired himself out to a rich farmer.

It was agreed between him and his master that he should work until the following spring, then he should receive his wages and would be free to leave. But the master set one condition.

"If one of us should lose his temper before spring comes," said the master, "he must pay a fine. If you get angry, you pay me a thousand silver coins. If I get angry, I pay you a thousand."

"Where would a poor fellow like me get so much money?" asked the elder brother.

"Don't worry about that. You can earn it by working for me ten more years."

At first the elder brother wanted to refuse. But then he thought it over and decided to accept the condition. "No matter what happens," he said to himself, "I shall keep my temper. And if the master gets angry, why, then he will have to pay me a thousand silver coins. That is a fine sum! What couldn't my brother and I do with a thousand silver coins!" So he agreed, and the two shook hands on it.

Early next morning the rich farmer sent his new hired man out into the field.

"Go out with your scythe," he said, "and work as long as it is light."

The field hand worked hard the whole day. He was heartily glad when dusk fell and he could return to the farmhouse to rest. But when he got there the farmer asked him:

"Why have you come back?"

"And why not?" asked the field hand. "You told me to work as long as it was light. But now the sun has set."

"Oh, no, this won't do at all," said the farmer. "I did indeed tell you to work as long as there was light. But if the sun has set, his sister, the moon, has risen. You must work by moonlight."

"Am I to have no rest at all?" asked the field hand, astonished.

"Are you getting angry?" the farmer wanted to know.

"Not at all," said the field hand quickly. "But I am very tired."

He was hardly able to move, but he remembered the agreement, and he went back to the field. He worked all night, until the moon set. But the moon had no sooner left the sky than the sun rose. The man could bear it no longer. He dropped to the ground, worn out.

"A curse on your field, your crops, and your money!" he gasped.

The words were barely out of his mouth when the farmer appeared, as if by magic.

"I see you have lost your temper," he said. "You remember our agreement. Either you pay me a thousand silver coins or you work for me ten more years."

The field hand did not know what to do. He had no money with which to pay the fine. But how could he undertake to work ten years for such a slave driver? At last he told the farmer that he would pay him the money as soon as he had earned it elsewhere. It was hard to make the farmer agree to this. But at last he let the poor man go to earn the sum by working in another place.

Tired, discouraged, empty-handed, the poor man returned home.

"How did you make out?" asked the younger brother.

The elder told him the whole story.

"What's to be done?" he asked, when he had finished. "Where shall I earn a thousand silver coins? And if I don't give the farmer the money soon, he will have me punished for not paying my debt."

"Don't take it to heart," said the younger brother. "You stay here and look after the house. I will go and hire myself out. I am young and strong. I can soon earn a good sum."

So the younger brother went off and hired himself out to the same rich farmer. The farmer wanted to set the same condition. If he lost his temper, he would pay the field hand a thousand silver coins and release him. If the field hand lost his temper, he would pay the farmer a thousand silver coins or work for ten years without wages.

"No," said the younger brother. "The sum is not large enough. If you get angry, you pay me two thousand silver coins. And the same holds for me, or I'll work twenty years without wages."

"That suits me capitally," said the rich, greedy farmer.

And so the younger brother entered his service.

When the sun rose early the next morning the young field hand was still asleep.

"Get up!" cried the farmer, prodding him. "It will be midday before you know it, and here you are still lying abed!"

"What's the matter?" asked the field hand, rubbing his eyes. "Are you angry at me?"

"Not at all," said the farmer hastily. "I only wanted to tell you that it's time to go out into the field and get in the crop."

"All right," drawled the field hand, yawning, and he got up, ever so slowly, and slowly began to draw on his clothes.

"Hurry, man, hurry! It's late!" cried the farmer.

"You're not angry, are you?" asked the field hand.

"No, no, I just want to remind you of the hour," said the farmer.

"That's all right, then. Only be sure to remember our agreement," said the field hand.

He dawdled so that it was nearly noon before he was ready to go out to the field.

"Is it worth while starting work now?" he asked the farmer. "You see, people are eating dinner at this hour. Let's sit down and have our dinner properly, too."

The farmer bit his lip with vexation, but he agreed, and they made a good meal. After dinner, as they were setting out for the field, the hired man turned to the farmer with a yawn.

"We are working people," he said. "It is only right that we should take a nap after dinner. Then we'll have more strength with which to work."

With that he lay down under a shady tree, fell asleep, and slept till evening.

"This is too much!" cried the farmer. He strode over to the field hand and shook him by the arm. "In heaven's name, wake up! Here it is already dusk and not a stroke of work have you done!"

"You're really angry with me, eh?" said the field hand sleepily.

"No, no. I'm not at all angry," replied the farmer, remembering his agreement. "I just wanted to tell you that it's getting dark and it's time to go home."

"Very well," said the field hand pleasantly, and returned to the house with his master.

When they reached the farmhouse, the farmer found a guest waiting for him. So he sent the hired man out to butcher a sheep, that he might prepare a feast for his guest.

"Which sheep shall I butcher?" asked the hired man.

"Any that comes your way," answered the farmer

hastily. He was happy to think that he was getting some work out of the man at last.

The hired man went off, and the farmer sat down with his guest for a good talk. Time passed, and the hired man did not return. The farmer began to grow uneasy. Suddenly he heard a clamor in the yard. It was crowded with neighbors; they were making a great to-do.

"Your hired man has lost his mind!" they cried. "He is butchering one sheep after another!"

The farmer rushed out to the sheep pen and saw that in truth the hired man had slaughtered the whole flock.

"What have you done, you good-for-nothing?" shouted the farmer. "Devil take you!"

"I only did what you ordered," answered the hired man quietly. "You told me to butcher any sheep that came my way. But you see, when one sheep came my way, all the rest followed. So I had to butcher them all. It's a pity, because now you are really angry."

"No, no!" insisted the farmer. "I'm not angry. I'm only sorry to see that you've done away with the whole flock."

"Oh, if you are not angry, I'll keep my part of the bargain and go on working for you until spring," said the hired man.

The farmer did not know whether to be glad or sorry about this. Indeed, during the next few months the hired man nearly drove him to despair. It was understood that they were to part in the spring as soon as they heard the first call of the cuckoo. But spring was still far off and the call of the cuckoo would not be heard for a long time. Finally the farmer thought up a scheme that would rid him of his unwanted helper.

He took his wife to the woods, had her climb a tree, and told her that as soon as she saw him again she should give the call of the cuckoo. Then he went home and told the hired man to fetch his gun: they were going hunting.

No sooner had they entered the woods than the farmer's wife saw them coming and began to call:

"Cuckoo, cuckoo, cuckoo!"

"Congratulations!" said the farmer. "The cuckoo is calling. That means your time is up."

But the hired man protested.

"Impossible!" he said. "A cuckoo calling in winter! I must fetch that bird down with a shot and see what sort it is."

He raised his rifle and took aim at the top of the tree where the farmer's wife was perched.

"Stop!" cried the farmer.

"I must shoot," insisted the man.

"Devil take you!" cried the farmer. "Will you never do what I want!"

"Ah, now you've lost your temper for fair," said the hired man.

"Temper or no temper, be off with you!" shouted the farmer.

"Gladly," answered the hired man. "But first you must give me the two thousand silver coins you promised me if you got angry before my time was up."

"Take your two thousand and get out," said the farmer. "Now I understand the saying: 'Don't dig a pit for another, lest you fall into it yourself.'"

So the younger brother got the two thousand silver coins and took them home. What cheer there was then in the little house! The elder brother was able to pay his debt to the greedy farmer, and the brothers still had a thousand silver coins on which to live happily for many a long day.

The Forty Whoppers

The Kazakh people live on the vast steppes, or grasslands, of central Asia. Nowadays they are settled on large farms, each worked by several families. Long ago, when they were ruled by princes called khans, they roamed the country with their sheep and goats and their herds of camels. They also raised horses and liked to drink fermented mare's milk. Below is a yarn that amused these Asiatic herdsmen. It is popular as well with neighbors of the Kazakhs: the Turkmen, natives of the semidesert region east of the Caspian Sea, who are also herdsmen and in addition grow cotton.

Once upon a time there lived a cruel khan. He was tired of feasting and of hunting and of all the

55

amusements at court. So he sent messengers far and wide over the land to proclaim that he desired a story-teller. Whoever would come to the palace and tell him forty whoppers, without a word of truth in them, would be rewarded with a bag of gold. But woe to the man who would falter in the telling and talk sense. He would be thrown into a pit and taken out only to be executed beyond the city wall.

As soon as the message was proclaimed, storytellers began to flock to the court. Some were driven there by greed for gold, some because they were so poor that they were desperate, and some because they thirsted for fame. But though many came, none met the khan's terms. One after another they met their end at the hands of the executioner. Finally there was no one left who was willing to try his luck at such a risk.

One day a boy knocked at the palace gate. He looked like a ragamuffin. He was barefoot. His clothes were in tatters, and his face was dirty.

"What do you want?" demanded the porter gruffly.

"I have come to tell the Khan forty whoppers," answered the boy.

The porter gave him a scornful stare and said roughly:

"Get out if you know what's good for you. Do you want your head chopped off?"

"No, I want a bag of gold," replied the boy briskly. "Take me to the khan."

When the porter saw that the boy was set on taking his chances, he finally let him in. After passing through many halls and corridors, the boy was finally admitted to the khan himself.

The khan lay sprawling on silken cushions. He was dying of boredom and very cross. The courtiers stood stock-still, fearing to call his wrath down on their heads by the slightest movement. They dared not so much as cough. The slaves who were bringing the khan food on golden dishes and drink in golden goblets walked on tiptoe, holding their breath. With a wave of his hand the khan put aside one dish after another. At his frown the servants trembled, and the courtiers turned pale with fear.

Seeing the tattered boy, the khan asked sternly:

"What do you want here?"

"O great Khan," answered the boy respectfully, "I have come to tell you forty whoppers."

The khan looked at the boy more closely and his eyes blazed fiercely.

"You rascal!" he exclaimed. "Do you want to lose your head?"

"No, indeed, great Khan," said the boy boldly. "I would like it better if you heard my stories and gave me a bag of gold."

The khan was amazed at the saucy boy. For a moment he was silent. Then in a voice thick with rage he said:

"Very well. Speak. I am listening."

"This all happened long ago," the boy began, "when the sky was no bigger than a saddle-pad and the earth no larger than a camel's footprint. I wasn't born yet. I made my living by herding my grandfather's horses.

"One hot day I drove the horses to water. But when I reached the river I found it frozen.

"I began to chop a hole in the ice with an axe, but only managed to nick the blade. Then I had a bright idea. I took off my head, and with all my might I knocked my forehead against the ice. And what do you think? I made such a huge hole that I watered a hundred horses.

"When the horses had drunk their fill, they began to graze on the ice. Without glancing at them I saw that my favorite brindled mare was missing.

"I struck my shepherd's crook into the ground, and climbing to the top of it, I began to look for my mare. But I saw nothing. Then I stuck a knife on top of the crook and climbed onto that. Still I saw nothing. In despair, I stuck a needle into the handle of the knife, and looked through the needle's eye. Only then I noticed my mare. She was standing on a tall rock in the middle of the sea and her colt was frisking about her in the waves.

"At once I turned my crook into a boat and my knife into an oar and sailed to fetch my mare. But when I reached the middle of the sea, I began to sink. I jumped onto the knife and used the crook for an oar instead, and sailed on without further trouble. Before I had drawn three breaths I was on the opposite shore.

"I lassoed the mare, mounted her, placed the colt before me across the saddle, and dashed back by sea. I was riding quietly, galloping over the waves and humming a song, when suddenly the mare stumbled on a rock. Again I felt myself sinking.

"What was I to do? The answer was easy: I jumped onto the back of the colt, set the mare across the saddle before me, and a moment later I reached the shore.

"In good time I arrived at the spot where I had left

my herd of horses. They were grazing among bushes of meadowsweet.

"No sooner did I tether the mare to the tallest bush than a hare jumped from under my feet. I ran after him, but he was faster than I. As I ran I snatched an arrow and shot it at the hare. It struck him plump in the chest but only bounced off. Then I took another arrow, being careful to shoot its blunt end first, and it went right through the hare.

"I skinned the hare, separated the fat from the meat, and began to collect dried dung to make a fire. Just then I noticed that the mare, thrashing her hoofs as if she were scared, was mounting into the air. I had tethered her to the neck of a swan by mistake.

"I dropped the pieces of dried dung onto the ground and ran to untie the mare. But as I did so, the dung itself spread wings and soared into the clouds: I had been gathering not dried dung but quails!

"Finally I managed to start a fire. I put the fat into a kettle without a nick in it and set the kettle over the flame. But the fat kept leaking out. I transferred the fat to a kettle full of holes and not a drop was lost. The fat was soon rendered down to the last drop. I poured the fat into a bag made out of a calf's stomach.

"Then I boiled the meat and was getting ready to eat it when I remembered that I had no head. I had left it near the hole in the ice.

"I almost cried. What could I do? Without stopping to think I began to shove the meat down my throat.

"When my stomach was full, I thought I had best use the fat to oil my boots. I oiled one boot, but there wasn't enough fat for the other one.

"Then I went to sleep. I was awakened by a loud noise: shots and yells and sounds of fighting. I opened my eyes and what did I see? My two boots were battling, one boot was belaboring the other and shouting: 'Take that and that, and that for good measure! The master oiled you and not me!'

"I tore the boots apart and said to the offended one:

"'Don't be so angry. It can't be helped: you were born unlucky.'

"And patting the fighters on the shoulder, I laid them to rest, one to the right of me, the other to the left. When I woke in the morning I found that the offended boot had disappeared.

"I put both feet into the remaining boot and started to run after the fugitive. I ran without rest for a day, for a month, for a year. At last I reached a village where a feast was being held. How it happened I don't know, but I was among the feasters.

"The servants were handing about platters of meat and other good things. And who do you suppose was among them, waiting on the guests? My lost boot!

"I called to him in amazement.

"The boot, hearing my voice, came over to me. But he was so afraid of being scolded for having run away that he almost dropped the platter he was holding. To put me into a good temper he served me one platter after another until I had consumed five platters of meat. And as sauce for my meat he said the same thing every time:

" 'You were too stingy to oil me, you mean thing! I'll pay you back properly. Here, you shall eat a whole platterful of meat.'

"He gave me so much food that I hadn't the strength to push it all down my throat. So I sent the other boot to fetch my head. He brought it. I put it on again, and ate more heartily than I had eaten in my whole life.

"Then, with both boots on my feet and my head on my shoulders, I returned to my horses. What with all the food I had eaten, and the heat of the day, I became very thirsty. I bent over the hole in the ice and began to drink. When I had drunk my fill I wanted to rise, but I couldn't budge. I didn't know why. Then I saw that while I had been drinking, sixty wild ducks and seventy drakes had frozen to my whiskers.

"What do I need so many ducks and drakes for? I said to myself. So I put them into a bag and exchanged them for a crane. But you must know, O great Khan, that this crane was larger than a dromedary. His beak was so long that he could drink from the deepest well without stooping."

"Perhaps the well wasn't so deep," said the khan, thinking that the boy was getting to the end of his whoppers and the time had come to decide whether or not to chop off his head.

"Maybe the well wasn't very deep," admitted the boy, "because if you threw a stone into it in the morning it would reach the bottom of the well by evening."

"Then perhaps the days were short ones," said the khan.

"Yes, perhaps the days were short," admitted the boy, "because a flock of sheep could cross the whole land from end to end in a single day."

The khan bit his lip in vexation, and the ragamuffin concluded:

"What I have told you, O great Khan, is what actually happened to me. But if I started to tell you all I've heard about what happened to others I would grow old before I finished."

The khan had to confess that he had never heard such a string of whoppers, so he ordered that the boy be given a bag of gold. But he was such a cruel old khan that he could not bear thinking that his terms had been met, and he died of vexation three days later.

The boy lived for many years and when he was an old grandfather he entertained his grandchildren with just such whoppers as he had told the khan. But they were such terrible whoppers that you wouldn't believe them.

A Sherlock Holmes of the Steppes

Here is another Kazakh story of a very different kind.

A man looking for a camel that was missing from his small herd fell in with another Kazakh who was traveling on horseback. The two greeted each other, glad to meet on the broad, lonely steppe. The horseman dismounted, and the pair sat down, took out their pipes, and had a friendly smoke.

"I'm missing one of my camels," said the herdsman gloomily.

"Is your camel blind in the left eye?" asked the horseman. "And has it no front teeth?"

"Yes, yes, that's quite right!" exclaimed the herdsman joyfully. "Where did you see it?"

"I never saw your camel in my life," said the horseman. "But yesterday on my way here I came on its tracks."

"A fine story!" cried the herdsman, angrily knocking the ashes out of his pipe. "You say you never saw my camel and yet you can tell me just what the beast looks like."

In short, he accused the horseman of having stolen the camel and of adding it to a herd of his own. Nothing would do but that the stranger should come with him to the nearest *cadi,* as a Kazakh judge is called.

When they came before the cadi, the horseman readily declared that he had seen the tracks of a camel that was blind in the left eye and had no front teeth.

"I know more than that about the creature," he added.

"Speak, then!" said the cadi.

"The camel was carrying two loads that balanced each other. On one side hung a barrel of honey, and on the other side hung a sack of wheat."

"Yes, yes, that's quite right," cried the herdsman. "There speaks the thief!"

The cadi, too, could not help believing that the horseman had stolen the camel and hidden it among his own herd. But he was a just judge who would not pronounce a verdict until he was certain of the truth.

"You claim you never laid eyes on that camel?" asked the cadi.

"Never," replied the horseman.

"How, then, do you know all you have told us about it?"

"Quite simple," said the horseman. "It is plain that the camel is blind in the left eye because the grass was nibbled only on the right side of the path."

"Very good," said the cadi. "But how do you know that it has no front teeth?"

"Quite simple," replied the horseman. "It is plain that the camel has no front teeth, because it takes strong front teeth to pull up, the camels' choicest tidbit: the prickly grass that was left untouched where it grazed."

"Very good," the cadi repeated. "But how do you know that the camel carried a barrel of honey balanced by a sack of wheat?"

"Quite simple," replied the horseman. "On one side of the path the flies were feasting on drops of honey, and on the other side the sparrows were hopping about pecking at fallen grains of wheat."

"Very good," said the cadi. "It is plain that you are not the thief."

"Quite plain," said the horseman.

"Quite plain," agreed the man whose camel was missing.

So the horseman was set free. Perhaps he helped the herdsman find his camel, a good beast even if it was blind in the left eye and had no front teeth. Besides, it was carrying a sack of wheat and a barrel of honey. But where and when it was found the story does not say.

The Cuckoo

Squat, black-haired folk, dressed in furs, these are the people whom the Russians used to call Samoyeds, but now they are known by the name they give themselves: Nenetz, meaning "man." There are very few of them, but they wander over a wide region along the Arctic coast of Europe and Asia. They move across the tundra, a great plain where only scrubby bushes grow, and if you drive a spade into the ground you strike frozen earth. In the spring the melting snow-water cannot sink into the icy ground, and it becomes marshy and infested with mosquitoes. Then the Nenetz travel north with their herds of reindeer and stay there until autumn. They live largely on raw meat and raw fish. The family makes its home in a tent shaped like a wigwam that is called a choom. *It is a framework covered with reindeer hide in winter and with birchbark in summer. Theirs is a hard life, as this story shows.*

Once there was a poor widow who had four wicked sons. They ran out and played in the snow all day

69

long and never did anything at all for their mother. When they came into the *choom,* the big tent with a smoke-hole at the top, they would track snow in with them, and their mother had to clean up after them. Their reindeer boots would be sopping wet and their mother would have to dry them carefully so they didn't get too stiff to draw on again. All this was very hard on the poor woman.

When she was not cooking for the boys or cleaning up the mess they had made, she was busy mending their torn clothes or making new ones for them. For, even though they wore hoods and jackets and boots of stout reindeer hide, they managed to get rips in them or to lose them. And the rest of the time the poor woman would stand on the riverbank fishing for the food for her lazy, hungry brood. It was very hard, and the boys gave her no help.

One day she was fishing very late in the cold and the wet and she got sick. She lay in the choom, unable to move, her cheeks hot with fever and her throat sore and dry.

"Fetch me a drink of water," she said to the boys. "My throat is so dry."

"My boots are off," said the oldest boy.

"I have lost my hood," said the second.

"I'm tired," said the third.

The fourth did not answer at all.

The mother lay quietly awhile, but her throat continued to trouble her.

"The river is so near," she said. "You don't need boots or a hood. Go fetch me a drink!"

But the boys paid no heed.

So the night went by and when morning came the boys ran out of the choom to play. They did not pay any attention to the poor woman.

After a while the oldest boy felt hungry and peeked into the choom to see if there was any food ready. But what he saw was so astonishing that he forgot all about his hunger.

There stood his mother in the middle of the choom putting on her cloak of reindeer skin. And the cloak, marvel of marvels, was covered with feathers!

Then the mother took the wooden board that she used to clean hides on, and the board turned into a bird's tail.

She put to her lips the thimble she used to sew her sons' clothes with, and it became a bird's beak.

She waved her arms and they turned into wings.

And then she rose up, in the shape of a bird, and flew out of the choom.

"Look, brothers!" cried the oldest boy. "Our mother is flying away!"

"Wait, Mother!" the boys cried in chorus. "Wait, and we'll fetch you a drink."

"Cuckoo, cuckoo," replied the mother. "It is too late. I am over the lake now. I am flying to the free waters."

Still the boys ran after her, and one of them held a pitcher, and all of them kept crying:

"Come home, Mother, come home! Here is water to drink. Come home!"

But the bird answered from afar:

"Cuckoo, cuckoo. It is too late. I shall not come back."

For days and nights the boys ran after their mother. They ran through the swamps and over the hillocks and on the hard rocks. They ran till their feet bled, and wherever they stepped they left a red trail on the tundra.

But from that day to this the mother cuckoo always abandons her children. From that day to this the mother cuckoo does not bother to build her own nest or to tend her own eggs or to raise her own brood.

And from that day to this, trailing across the tundra, you will find a red moss.

The Greedy Rich Man

In the foothills of the Ural Mountains in eastern Russia dwell the Votyaks (the native name is Udmurt). Their land is thickly forested and their mountains are rich in ores, so that many Votyaks are lumberjacks and miners. Others are farmers, raising crops of rye, oats, and flax. This story must have been first told by them.

Once upon a time there was a rich man who was very greedy. He ate a lot. He drank a lot. He slept a lot. But work he did not, not even a little. Instead, he hired men to work for him while he was eating and drinking and sleeping.

He had only one worry. He was troubled because the day was too short. With such a short day, how could his laborers get enough work done? If only, he said to himself, I could make the day longer! What plowing and planting and harvesting, what digging and building they would do for me then! True, I am rich. But if the day were only longer, how very rich I would be!

So he went in search of a wise man who could tell him how to make the day longer. Finally he found such a wise man. He was as poor as he was wise. His name was Lopsho Pedun.

"What trouble has brought you to my house?" asked Lopsho Pedun. So rich a guest could come for nothing but advice.

"I am troubled because the day is too short," answered the greedy one. "Even in summer the day is shorter than a hare's tail. No sooner do my laborers take up their tools than the hens begin to perch for the night. And summer is the best time for work. Pray teach me, O wise one, how to make the summer day longer."

Lopsho Pedun looked at the greedy man with sly eyes, and said:

"I will teach you how to lengthen the summer day. But you must do exactly as I tell you."

74

"Thank you, O wise one," answered the rich man. "Only tell me, and I will do just as you say."

"Well, then," said Pedun, "go home and put on seventy-seven garments, and each garment must be good and warm. On top of these you must wear a heavy greatcoat. On your head you must have a fur cap. On your feet you must have woollen socks and thick felt boots. Then take a large bag full of provisions and carry it on your shoulders. And in your hand take a wooden pitchfork. When you have done all this, walk until you come to a tall birch tree and climb to the top. Lift up your pitchfork and hook the sun with it, and hold the sun steadily in one spot like a golden pancake. Then the sun will not be able to set, and the summer day will not come to an end."

"Good," said the rich man. "I will do just as you say. And in reward for your advice, here is a hundred rubles."

The poor wise man accepted the hundred rubles with a smile, and the greedy rich man went home to lengthen the summer day.

When he got home he put on seventy-seven warm garments, as the wise man had bidden him, and over them he put on a greatcoat. He set a fur cap on his head, and put woollen socks and thick felt boots on his feet. Then he piled a large bag of provisions on his shoulders, took a pitchfork in his hand, and went off to look for a tall birch tree. When he came to the tree he shifted the bag on his back, grasped the pitchfork firmly, and climbed to the top. It was not long before he managed to hook the sun with his pitchfork. And there he perched at the top of the tree, holding the sun aloft.

"Hey, there!" he shouted to his laborers. "See that you don't quit until sundown."

For an hour the rich man crouched at the top of the tree, clad in his seventy-seven warm garments and his greatcoat and his fur cap and his woollen socks and felt boots, holding the sun on his pitchfork. It was hot. Another hour passed, and he was still there. It was very hot. The greedy man's arms were numb from holding the sun on the pitchfork. His feet were swollen with heat. His shoulders ached from the heavy bag of provisions. His body seemed to be on fire.

Suddenly he let go of the pitchfork. It got caught in the branches of the birch tree and the sun fell out of it. The greedy rich man wanted to climb down from the tree, but his arm was lame from holding the pitchfork and he could barely stir. When he tried to move, he

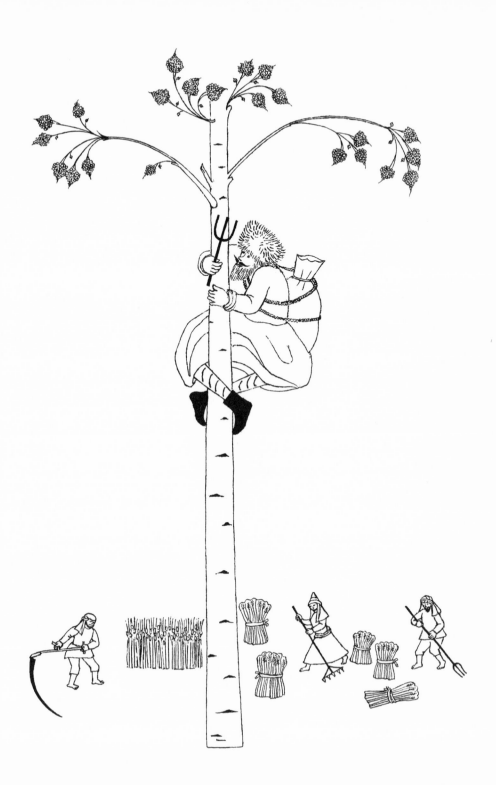

tumbled, plop! onto the ground. Luckily, he fell on his back on top of the bag of provisions. Luckily, he wore a fur cap, heavy socks, and fur boots. Luckily, he was dressed in seventy-seven garments and a greatcoat. Otherwise he would have broken every bone in his body. As it was, he was only a little bruised.

He picked himself up, and as quickly as he could he too off the greatcoat and all but two of the seventy-seven garments. Oofff! he felt better. Now he knew why the poor wise man, Lopsho Pedun, had smiled at his question. Greedy as he was, and rich as he was, he must be content with a summer day that was no longer than a summer day. It was worth the hundred rubles that he had given Lopsho Pedun to learn that. So he went home.

He left the seventy-five garments where he had thrown them for any poor wayfarers to find. He left the bag of provisions to the small beasts of the field and the birds of the air. He was poorer by a hundred rubles, but he was richer in wisdom. His laborers had reason to be grateful to Lopsho Pedun. And the wise man smiled a wider smile than before.

The Girl in the Moon

On the vast frozen plains, or tundras, and in the forests of eastern Siberia live the Yakuts. They are a tough people, fit for the hardships of their severe surroundings. They herd the reindeer who provide them with food and clothing. They fish and trap fur-bearing animals. The Yakut house is a square, one-room cabin built of upright logs that are freshly plastered with dung and clay every year. The flat roof extends over the cattle shed next to the cabin. In the center of the single room is an open fireplace. Here the Yakuts do their modest cooking. Here they gather to listen to such a tale as this.

O nce upon a time there was a little orphan girl who had no relatives to take care of her. There she was, all alone in the poor one-room hut. Her father had left her a quiet old horse and a lone calf. She sold the horse, and for the money that she got she bought a few bricks of tea. The calf she had to slaughter for meat. When the meat was eaten, she had nothing but the bricks of tea. These she bartered for some fish. But when she had eaten the fish, the poor orphan did not know what to do.

She had some old fishing nets that had belonged to her father, but she did not know how to use them properly. Besides, wicked folk would secretly remove the few fish that were caught in the old, torn nets, so that she had nothing at all to eat.

Then the neighbors came together to talk over what should be done for her. Many kettlefuls of tea were drunk and endless words were said, but no one was willing to take care of her. Finally the head man said that he would take her into his hut.

"Let her live with us, and do the work for us," he said. "In return I will feed her and clothe her. There will always be some scraps for her in my house, and besides, her father was a friend of mine."

That same day the head man set the orphan girl on his horse, mounted behind her, and took her to his house.

But the poor girl's lot was a sad one. She had to carry

great skinfuls of water, to cut wood in the forest and drag it to the hut. She had to milk the cow, and do all the hard work. When her load of wood was too heavy to carry, and she dropped and scattered it, or when she brought skins of water only half full, the head man would scold her and his wicked old wife would give her a beating. She was treated so cruelly that she watered all her work with her tears.

One winter night it was so cold that the earth cracked with a noise like the sound of the medicine man's drum. In spite of the cold, the poor orphan was sent out to fetch some water from a hole in the ice of a nearby lake. She took with her a heavy crowbar with a wooden handle. When she got to the lake, she broke the ice with the crowbar and dipped her skin bottles into the hole to fill them with water. Then she set a full skin on either end of the yoke that she carried on her shoulders, and started on her way back to the hut.

She was nearly home when she stumbled against a willow tree and spilled the water on the frozen ground. What was she to do? She could not go all the way back to the lake. Besides, she had been told to hurry home in order to finish some work that was waiting for her in the house. But she was afraid to return with empty skins: the chief's wicked wife was sure to give her a terrible beating.

The poor orphan began to cry. It was so cold that the tears froze on her cheeks, but there was no one to witness her grief. For miles around neither man nor beast was to be seen. Every living thing had hidden from the frost. The wild creatures were huddled in their caves. The cows were in their sheds. The men were crouched over their hearth fires.

And the frost was increasing. From far away you could hear muffled sounds like peals of thunder: it was the ice on the lake cracking in the cold. The silence of the night made the noise all the more fearful. The poor girl beat her hands together and cried.

Only the moon saw her tears. He saw her and pitied her, and he loved her for her beauty.

At last the poor orphan, fearing that she would freeze to death, lifted her eyes to the moon and begged:

"Moon, Moon, come and take me away! I have neither father nor mother. There is not a hut in all our village where they would let me warm myself quietly by the fire. Have pity on me, O Moon! Take me away!"

No sooner had she spoken than the moon fell at her feet.

Now the sun had also heard the girl's prayer, and he was so taken with her beauty that he rolled out of the sky and dropped at her feet beside the moon.

At once a fight began between the sun and the moon as to which of them was to be the girl's rescuer. The poor girl was so frightened that she held on to a branch of the willow tree to keep herself from falling.

The fight went on for some time. But it was an unequal one. The sun was stronger, and he overpowered the moon.

Nevertheless the moon had a word to say:

"Brother Sun, after all, it was not to you that this girl cried for help, but to me. Let me take her away!"

But the sun refused to listen.

Then the moon began pleading with the sun.

"O great Sun," he begged, "let me take the girl! You walk the sky by day, and on a short winter day you have not long to travel. But I must roam the sky all through the long winter night, and it is very dull without a companion. I look down at the earth chained by the cold, and it saddens me. Give me the girl!"

Still the sun would not listen to him.

Finally the moon said:

"Brother Sun, you are the older and the stronger.

But consider: you are so hot that you will surely scorch the poor girl. And what will become of her then?"

At that the sun could not help but agree that it was best for the orphan to go to the moon. So the moon promptly seized her, together with the willow branch to which she was clinging, and lifted her into the sky with him.

And now, if you look up at the moon on a clear night, you will see the girl with the yoke on her shoulders, holding on to the willow branch. Only sometimes, as she remembers her sorrows, or when, looking down at the earth, she sees more evil than good, she hides herself in misery. Then the moon, who loves her dearly, grows black with grief, and men say that the moon is eclipsed. But the girl soon returns to her friend, and at once the face of the moon lights up with joy. The poor orphan girl, who was treated so cruelly on earth, rejoices with her friend. She will live with him happily as long as the moon exists, and as long as there is a sky through which they may travel together.

A Time for Everything

In old Russia it was not only the simple people who liked to listen to stories. Rich merchants and landowners and even the czars themselves would have their own storytellers, who were often blind men. Ivan the Terrible had among his servants three blind men whose duty it was to come to his bedside, one after another, and tell him stories until he fell asleep. Perhaps this is one that amused the Czar.

Once there was a poor widow who had only one son. He was not very little, but he was not very big either.

One morning she called him to her and said:

"Child, it is time that you stopped hanging onto my

apron strings. You must go out and see what is to be seen. You must rub elbows with people. That is the way to learn."

"Go out and rub elbows with people?" repeated the boy.

"Just so, my darling," said his mother, and with a little shove she sent him out-of-doors.

The boy wandered off and before long he came to a threshing ground. Men and women were busily using their flails, making the chaff fly. The good grain they piled into carts.

The boy stepped right in among the threshers and went from one to another, his arms akimbo, carefully rubbing elbows now with this one and now with that.

It is not easy to use a flail when someone is just at your elbow, and rubbing it into the bargain. The threshers, at first astonished, soon grew angry.

"What are you doing? Be off with you!" they cried.

The boy did not stop rubbing elbows, however, for he remembered what his mother had told him. So they began using their flails on his back, and they spanked him hard and long till the tears came. It was plain that he was not wanted here.

He ran home to his mother, and the tears were still wet on his cheeks as he shot through the door.

"Child, child, what has happened to you?" cried his mother.

So he told her the story.

"Ah, my chick, you should not have done that!" said his mother sadly. "You should have taken a flail and threshed the buckwheat with the others. And then they would have been glad of your company. Or, if you had no flail, you should have cheered them on and wished them well. They might even have given you some buckwheat and I would have cooked it for you and put a lump of fat into it. We would have had a good meal. You should have said to them: 'Good! Good! May you have this load and more, too! May there be no end to your carting!' "

"Is that what I should have said?" asked the boy.

"Just so, my darling!" said his mother.

By the next day the boy had got over his beating and he wandered off again.

The first thing he met was a funeral procession. The mourners marched along slowly, with bowed heads, behind the cart on which the coffin was being carried.

The boy ran up to them and called out in a clear voice:

"Good! Good! May you have this load and more, too!"

87

The mourners stopped in their tracks, astonished. The cart with the coffin halted.

"Good! Good!" cried the boy. "May there be no end to your carting!"

At this the mourners cried out, not with grief but with anger. And one of them, a tall, sturdy man, turned on the boy and gave him a thorough spanking. It was plain to him that he was not wanted here.

He ran home to his mother, and the tears were still wet on his cheeks as he shot through the door.

"Child, child, what has happened to you?" asked his mother.

So he told her the story.

"Ah, my chick, you should not have done that!" said his mother sadly. "You should have taken off your cap and crossed yourself. You should have wept for the good old man that was gone. You should have lifted up your voice and cried: 'Oh, the pity of it! Oh, the pity!' Then they would have taken you with them in the procession and afterward you would have been invited to the funeral feast. You would have filled your stomach with pancakes and other good things, and maybe even brought some home in your pockets for me. You should have wept and wailed."

"Wept and wailed?" repeated the boy.

"Just so, my darling," said his mother.

By the next day the boy had got over his beating and he wandered off again. Before long he came upon another procession. His eyes brightened, for this was much finer than the first, and ever so jolly. It was a wedding procession. The bride and groom and the parents of the groom, and their sisters and their brothers and their cousins and their aunts and their uncles, all gaily dressed in their best, were marching along to the playing of pipes and accordions.

The boy stared for a moment in wonder. Then he went up to the wedding party, and keeping step with the bride, he began to weep and to wail.

"Oh, the pity of it!" he cried.

The bride stopped in her tracks, astonished. And the rest of the procession: the groom, and the old people and the young people, and the pipers and the accordion players stopped, too.

Thereupon the boy wailed more loudly than before:

"Oh, the pity of it! Oh, the pity!"

At this the groom's father, a great bearded man, seized the boy and gave him a box on the ear that made it sting.

"What bad luck are you bringing on this pair! The pity of it, indeed! You'll be needing pity, you idiot!"

It was plain to the boy that he was not wanted here.

He ran home to his mother, and his ear still stung as he shot through the door.

She heard his story through, and then she said sadly:

"Ah, my chick, you should not have done that! You should have taken a pipe with the others, and gone dancing and piping with them along the road. Then you would have seen the fine doings at church and you would have been invited to the wedding feast. You would have filled your stomach with bride-cake, and perhaps taken some home in your pockets for me."

"I should have piped and danced?" repeated the boy.

"Just so, my darling," said his mother.

By the next day the boy was ready to wander off once more.

After he had trotted quite a distance he noticed a cloud of smoke off to the right, and hastening his steps, he came to a burning barn. The peasant whose barn was on fire kept throwing pailfuls of water onto the flaming timbers, but the barn was of wood, after all, and filled with dry hay, and the buckets of water did not move as fast as the wind that made the blaze greater.

The boy pulled a hollow reed out of his pocket and began leaping about in a kind of dance, and piping the merriest tune he knew.

When the peasant noticed the boy apparently rejoicing at his misfortune, he got so angry that he wasted a whole pail of water on him. The boy was drenched to the skin. Clearly he was not wanted here.

He ran home, dripping wet, and some of the water was salt because it came from his eyes.

"Child, child, what has happened?" cried his mother.

So he told her the story.

"Ah, my chick, you should not have done that," she said sadly, as she rubbed him and patted him, and brought out some dry clothes. "You should have taken a bucket of water and thrown it on the burning barn. Yes, indeed, a bucket of water was what was needed."

"A bucket of water?" repeated the boy.

"Just so, my darling," said his mother. "Now are you quite dry again?"

The boy nodded.

"Then run along and don't bother me while I cook dinner. Here's a piece of bread to eat on the way." And she sent him out-of-doors again with a little shove.

The boy set off, munching his bread and looking

about him as he walked. He had swallowed his last crumb when he came to a farmyard. The farmer had just finished slaughtering a hog. He had placed the hog on a spit over a fire so as to singe off its bristles before preparing it for meat. The fire was just beginning to burn nicely. Just then the farmer's wife came from the well carrying a wooden yoke on her shoulders, with a bucket of water suspended at either end of the yoke.

The boy did not hesitate a moment. He leaped for a bucket and poured the water over the fire where the farmer was singeing the hog.

The farmer did not hesitate a moment. He seized the boy and spanked him long and hard.

It was clear to him that he was not wanted here. He ran home to his mother, and he was still crying as he shot through the door.

"Child, child, what has happened to you now?" she exclaimed.

So he told her the story.

"Ah, my chick, you should not have done that," she sighed.

"But you said . . ." the boy began, when his mother interrupted:

"There is a time for everything: a time to throw

water on the fire and a time to let it burn, a time to weep and a time to dance, a time when we wish carts would carry their loads endlessly and a time when we wish there were no load at all. Oh, my chick, my child, my darling, when will you learn what the right time is?"

"I don't know, Mother," answered the boy slowly, "but I know what time it is now."

"Yes?" asked his mother eagerly.

"Time for dinner," said the boy.

And so it was.